MAKE TODAY BETTER THAN TOMORROW

PRANAY GUPTA

Copyright © Pranay Gupta
All Rights Reserved.

The Power full journey

Contents

Contents

Dear Reader

Before you start reading, let me tell you that I am not gifted with the art of crafting ab imaginary world.

So, my poetry is strictly based upon my day-to-day experiences.

I was born and raised in Delhi and later in my high school days my family and I finally settled down in Sarita Vihar.

What I have written is not necessary that you just want to read it, that you understand it, everyone takes the story, but no one can learn from it and you were found to be a learner when you yourself felt that story and lived in life. There is no time to learn anything, but we learn a new thing every day, live a new life, what I learned, I am telling in my words that I want you to learn this lesson then people reach then one thing is not necessary. As you think in life, sometimes real life is very different from these words, so always be happy in life and make people around you happy for two moments of life.

Regards! Have a good read!

• X •

Note From Author

Whenever I write a new book, a voice comes from inside. In such a big world, who read my book, then again there is a voice from inside, in such a big world there will be someone who will read my book.

There are only two sides to a coin in life, I can do this work, or I cannot do this work, now it depends on you whether you trust the side of the coin.

Thank you to all of you who made me reachable here and always kept my morale up. I am proud of my family, friends, and India's traditions who have always supported me.

CHAPTER ONE

Three laughing Monks

That was a long time ago. Three Monks lived in the North Privacy of old China. No one knows the names of those three. Because those three never talked about themselves and never answered anything. In China, they were simply known as the 3 Laughing Monks. All three of them used to do only one thing, entered any village, stood in the middle of the market, and started laughing, they used to laugh with their whole existence and the attention of the people themselves would be drawn towards them and gradually their A large crowd would gather all around. The whole village would start laughing seeing that Monks laughed with their concentration, engrossment, or completeness. When that village was submerged in the sea of laughing, they would leave for another village.

They neither spoke anything, did not preach nor taught anything. wherever they went they just laughed Wherever he went, he would create such an atmosphere with his laughter that people would forget all the sorrow and pain and start laughing only.

Slowly the people of China started liking them all and they started becoming famous all over China in the name of 3 Laughing Monks.

The people of China loved him very much. Before and even after him, no one preached like this "life should be just a laugh and nothing else". He didn't laugh at anyone in particular. He just laughed as if he understood the cosmic joke as if he understood the joke of God, and without using a single word, he spread so much joy throughout China that no one before today. Laughing at people all over China. With time, all three of them got old and one night while they were staying in the village, one of them died. The whole village was stunned, the whole village was expecting because they thought that whenever one of them dies, the other two will definitely cry, it will be worth watching because no one had ever seen these people crying. When morning came, the whole village gathered. But both the monks standing beside the dead body of the third were laughing loudly as if they had never laughed before today. Some elders of the village tried to make him understand that this was your companion, and you should not laugh at his death. Then that day those Monks spoke to the people for the first time and said that we were laughing because this man has won, we always wondered which of us died first. But this man defeated us by dying first. We are laughing at our defeat or its victory. Apart from this, it has been with us for many years. We laughed together, we enjoyed each other's presence, what better way to give him the last farewell than this. We can only laugh.

But the whole village was sad. When the dead monk's body was laid on the pyre for the last rites, all the villagers realized that the remaining two monks were not just joking. The third one who was dead was also laughing.

It was a custom in China that when a person died, his old clothes were taken off, he was washed and dressed in new clothes. But before dying, that third monk had asked his companions not to change clothes. The third monk said "Don't bathe me and don't change my clothes because I have never been impure. My life laughed so much that no impurity could have accumulated. I haven't accumulated any dust. Laughter is always fresh." That's why don't change my clothes by bathing. When the third monk's body was set on fire, the villagers came to know that the monk had hidden Chinese firecrackers in his old clothes before dying. Which exploded after the fire and spread colorfully in the sky. And seeing this, the whole village started laughing loudly, so even after the death of that third monk, the whole village was laughed at. Seeing all this, both the monks said that clever man, you are dead, but you defeated us once again and because of you this laughter was the last time on the faces of the villagers.

There is cosmic laughter which comes into existence when the whole joke of this universe is understood. which is of the highest. And only a Buddha can laugh like that

If you want to laugh, then laugh at yourself

CHAPTER TWO

Emperor Bu

It is a very famous story. About 1500 years ago, a Buddhist monk lived in India. His name was Bodhidharma, in the history of the entire Buddhist religion, after Gautam Buddha, if there has been any most influential and famous Buddhist monk, then it was only Bodhidharma. After Gautam Buddha, Bodhidharma spread Buddhism the most. It was Bodhidharma who took Buddhism from India to China. Which later came to be known as ZEN Buddhism. And then it spread through China to Japan, Korea, and many countries of Southeast Asia. The emperor who was in China at that time was named "Bu". Emperor Bu had heard a lot about Gautam Buddha and his thoughts of peace. And he was very much influenced by them too. It is said that the emperor kept waiting for years that a Buddhist monk from India should come to China after crossing the inaccessible valleys of the great Himalayas. And he should tell him about his wisdom and his thoughts. When Bodhidharma reached China, the old emperor Bu came to meet him. At that time Emperor Bu was going through the problem of his mental disturbance.

Emperor Bu said to Bodhidharma - I tried a lot but there is no peace in my mind. It keeps wandering all the time can you calm my pride

Bodhidharma said - Where is your troubled mind. Let me calm it down now.

Emperor Bu did not understand anything and stood silently.

Bodhidharma said - OK, I will calm your mind, but for this you will have to come to me tomorrow morning at 4 AM and yes remember to bring your disturbed mind with you.

Emperor Bu found this answer somewhat strange. He kept thinking about sleep the whole night, what a crazy monk is, says to bring your mind with you. Spear mind is also some stuff which I will leave and come.

He has decided many times that there is no point in being now. The man seems insane. But he had no other way. That's why he decided that he must go to that monk once.

The next morning at 4 o'clock Emperor Bu reaches Bodhidharma. Bodhidharma was sitting in meditation with his eyes closed. Bodhidharma opens his eyes on hearing the arrival of the emperor. And the emperor tells Bu, then you come. Flame now quickly give me your troubled mind, let me calm it down and give it back to you.

Emperor Bu said - What are you talking about? Is there any object of the mind which I should give to you, it is inside me, it is inside the two bones of my head.

Bodhidharma said - So one thing is clear from this that your mind is inside you.

The emperor said - yes, my mind is inside me.

Bodhidharma said - Then you close your eyes and sit down and find that disturbed mind within you. As soon as you find your disturbed mind, let me know and I will calm it down.

This answer of Bodhidharma also seemed strange to Emperor Bu, but what could he have done. He closed his eyes and started looking at the thoughts arising in his mind. He kept trying to find his troubled mind. The more he went in, the more he failed to find his disturbed mind. A few hours passed; the sun had come out Emperor Bu opened his eyes.

Bodhidharma asked - Got your disturbed mind?

Emperor Bu nodded his head.

Bodhidharma said - okay come again tomorrow morning and try to find your mind again

Emperor Bu leaves from him.

The next morning at 4 o'clock Emperor Bu comes again to Bodhidharma. Bodhidharma again asks the emperor to close his eyes and sit down. Emperor Bu again closes his eyes and tries to find his troubled mind. The more he goes on drowning in himself, the more he gets away from his mind and his thoughts, today Emperor Bu was sitting in the afternoon, now he opened his eyes

Bodhidharma asked - Got your disturbed mind?

The emperor nodded his head again.

The next day at 4 o'clock in the morning Emperor Bu again comes to Bodhidharma. Bodhidharma again asks the emperor to sit with his eyes closed. Emperor Bu again closes his eyes and starts trying to find his disturbed mind. Today it becomes evening for Emperor Bu to sit down.

While leaving, Bodhidharma asked - Have you found your disturbed mind today?

The emperor nodded his head again.

Bodhidharma said - OK, come again tomorrow morning.

The next day Emperor Bu arrives at 3 in the morning. Sitting down and trying to find his disturbed mind, the whole day passes, the whole night passes, but Emperor Bu keeps searching for his disturbed mind with his eyes closed. Bodhidharma also sits next to Emperor Bu. The more he went down inside himself, the more he failed to find his mind. He understood that there is nothing like mind inside, it is only a group of thoughts which we call mind. If there is thought then there is mind, if there is no thought then there is no mind. When there is nothing like mind inside, nothing can be done about it. What we call mind, it is only those thoughts which keep arising in us in our unconscious state, if we come to our consciousness and start living consciously, then this thought remains nothing like it. And when there is no thought, then there is no mind. Now he understood why Bodhidharma was repeatedly telling him to give your mind to me. Because he knew that there is no such thing as the mind.

Emperor Bu opened his eyes.

Bodhidharma asked- Got your disturbed mind?

The emperor said - I did not get a disturbed mind, but that peace was definitely found. What I was looking for, till I did not look for the mind, I used to be very upset. When I searched, I found that there is nothing like the mind.

Bodhidharma said - Whenever you feel unrest, then sit down with your eyes closed and look inside yourself that where is this disturbance and you will not find any disturbance in you, but yes whenever you look, you will definitely find such a person inside you. Which is very calm and stable? As Emperor Bu realized, the mind is nothing but the thoughts within us. We can control our mind by controlling our thoughts.

If we see in our life, there are lakhs of people around us who are troubled by mental disturbance. They all want to come out of this mental disturbance, but they do not know how to come out of it and if some people even try to come out of it, some give up because of initial failure and then this mental disturbance Stays with them till death. Many times, mental thoughts are more painful than body pain and it makes the life of a person very difficult, people go through this mental disturbance because they never try to see the mind, they never glimpse inside themselves. Do not try to see what the real cause of this mental unrest is.

As we saw in the above story that there is no such thing as mind in us. Actually, the mind is a group of thoughts arising inside us. Because we are thinking about anything in an unconscious way.

Sometimes we think about the past, sometimes we think about the future. In the run-up to these thoughts, we have forgotten that life is neither in the past nor in the future, life is in today, it is in this moment which we have stopped living. If we learn to live in our conscious state, become aware and start walking in the thoughts going on inside us, then gradually the thoughts arising in us will decrease. Because then the thoughts do not get time to arise. Because our mind thinks more only when it is in an unconscious state. Therefore, as our awareness increases, the speed of our thoughts becomes less and when we become silent then our mind disappears, and it is not a problem for us but happiness and becomes a source of peace. goes. That's why whenever you feel unrest or any kind of misery in your life, then sit quietly with your eyes closed and start watching the thoughts arising inside you, do not try to stop these rising thoughts, just let them come. And let it go and don't get entangled in these thoughts. You just see them as if you are standing on the side of a road and watching the vehicles coming and going, the same thoughts will come and go, you just have to keep looking at them. With time these thoughts will stop coming and you will eventually find yourself as someone who is quite stable and calm inside.

CHAPTER THREE

How to control your anger

Once upon a time, Gautam Buddha was sitting under a tree with his disciples, when one of his disciples asked, in fact, how can we control our anger.

Gautam Buddha said that for this I will tell you a story, after listening to this story, you have learned to control your anger.

After this Gautam Buddha starts narrating his story. There lived a quarrelsome woman in a village. She often gets angry over small

things. And in anger would abuse anyone and hear good and bad, but after some time her anger subsided, she would regret her actions, all the members of her family were very upset with this angry attitude of her. There was always an atmosphere of fighting and unrest in that house. Due to the angry attitude of that woman, even her neighbors did not bother her, and that woman also understood that no one liked her because of her angry attitude. But even after wanting to get angry, she could not stop herself from speaking her words. One day a sage comes to that woman's door to ask for alms, after giving alms to the monk, that woman tells her problems with a very disappointed heart.

She says - Monk, I get angry very quickly and I cannot control my anger even if I want to. Please tell me about some remedy by which I can control my anger. That monk listens to the words of that woman very carefully and then after thinking for some time, takes out a vial full of medicine from his bag and gives it to that woman and says listen to me carefully, it will help to control anger. It is the best medicine. From now on whenever you get angry and feel like saying something abusive to someone, then put 4 drops of this medicine on your tongue and do not open your mouth for at least 10 minutes and if you open your mouth before 10 minutes then that medicine It will have no importance and it will not be able to show its effect.

Saying this, Monk leaves from there.

After this the woman starts using the medicine as per the instructions of Monk. Whenever she got angry, she would keep 4 drops of that medicine in her tongue and keep that medicine in her mouth for at least 10 minutes and then take it inside. After doing this process for the next 15 days, the woman gets rid of the habit of getting angry and then after a month when the monk comes again to her door to take alms. So, she runs and grabs the feet of those monks and says Monk, your medicine has cast a spell on me. Due to the effect of your medicine, now I do not get angry on talk and now there is an atmosphere of peace in my family too. Now I am very happy Monk. Hearing this from the woman's mouth, the monk smiles and says - Daughter, there was no medicine for anger in that bottle, but that bottle was just filled with water. You have found control over your anger not because of that medicine but because of keeping quiet.

After this Gautam Buddha becomes silent and then pauses for a while and says that anger can be controlled only by remaining silent. Because in anger, a person spews bad words from his mouth, which gives rise to new quarrels and troubles. That's why keeping silence due to anger is the only way to control anger, dear reader, we get angry on many small things in our life and lose our temper and then regret it later. I wish I had not got angry, when a person is angry, then his mind stops working. Only his mouth is speaking and then many times in anger, a person utters such words which he will regret for the rest of his life. Many times, under the control of anger of a few minutes, a person not only does mental valance, but he also does dangerous physical violence at times. Then the result of which he has to suffer throughout his life. Whereas anger was only for a few minutes. If we can stay calm on those few moments of anger, then we can end many fights and problems in our life before it even starts. So now whenever you get angry next time, keeping your mind calm, put a few drops of that medicine inside your mouth and keep your mouth closed for some time and you will be saved from some problems to come.

CHAPTER FOUR

OLD CLOTHES

Once a disciple of Gautama Buddha who was coming to Gautama Buddha's ashram for years. He would listen to her discourses, meditate in the ashram, and then go home, but for a few days he had stopped coming to the ashram. Gautam Buddha had also experienced this thing. One day when Gautam Buddha was returning after asking for alms from him, there was also the house of that disciple on the way, when Buddha had gone inside him, the person was doing some work in the courtyard. On seeing the Buddha, he quickly stood up with folded hands, he gave Buddha some water to drink and laid a mat on the platform of the courtyard for him to sit on. Buddha sat comfortably on the mat, then Buddha asked that disciple, is everything fine in your family? The disciple said yes everything is fine. Buddha asked then why did you stop coming to the ashram. Hearing this, the disciple started getting a little embarrassed and said now how can I tell you.

Gautam Buddha said that you can say without hesitation. The disciple said that my clothes have become old, it has become fat from many places, holes have come out in them, now they are not worth wearing at all There were some holes, after this Buddha stood up and smilingly put his hand on the disciple's shoulder and said, don't worry, everything will be fine. At the time of evening, when all the disciples from the ashram were going back home after listening to Buddha's discourses, Buddha asked one of his rich disciples to stop when everyone left. Buddha alone asked his rich disciple to give two pairs of clothes to that poor disciple. . That rich disciple leaves after promising to give clothes to that poor disciple. The next day that rich disciple gets two pairs of clothes for each member of that poor disciple's family in a bundle and sends it to his servant. Seeing whom the whole family of that poor disciple is very happy. The next day, when that poor disciple comes again to listen to Buddha's discourses, at the end, while leaving, Buddha stops that disciple and asks. Are you comfortable in your new clothes, do you need anything else? The disciple said that first of all thank you very much and I am comfortable in these clothes, and I do not want anything. Buddha asks when you have received new clothes, then what did you do with your old clothes. The disciple said that from now on our family will use them for laying and covering them in the bed, then Buddha said then what did you do with your old bed linen? The disciple said that I have changed the old window screen Buddha said so did you throw away your old screen? The disciple said no, now I am cutting the curtains into small pieces and using them to unload and hold hot utensils in the kitchen. Buddha asked, then what did you do with the kitchen clothes? The disciple said that now I will use them to wipe the house. Then Buddha asked what happened to your old mop? The disciple said that the old mop had become so wired that nothing could be done for it, so I made a lamp and gave some to the ashram so that the light of light could increase in the ashram. Hearing this, Buddha was very happy because he was commanded to understand that his disciple knows to appreciate clothes and he knows what is the value of any item.

Buddha always teaches that if you have anything which is more than what you need, then that thing should be given to the needy and that thing should be appreciated by the feet.

CHAPTER FIVE

WHEEL OF TIME

A fakir was going towards the city, so he was tired, and it was a light night. The city was still enough, the fakir came and stopped near a house. The one whose house was named "Shankar", Shankar was a kindhearted person and a very settled person. When Shankar saw the fakir, he brought the fakir to the house and did a lot of services, the fakir was very happy. Shankar said you should take this rest, as soon as it was morning, Shankar sent him away by giving him some grains and fruits. Here the fakir was very happy with Shankar's service and started praying, "May God bless you more and may God always be happy. Hearing the fakir's words, Shankar started laughing and said, oh my fakir, whatever I have now, I don't even have to live." After hearing this, the fakir kept looking at Shankar and started thinking in his mind that why he is saying this. Thinking so much, the fakir said that I would definitely meet you once while returning from the city, after saying so much, the fakir left from there. Exactly a year later, when the fakir saw that all his wealth, all his wealth was really gone. Then the fakir came to know that now Shankar is working as a servant in the house of a big landlord in a village outside Nagar. Shankar is living happily by building a small hut separately. He gets his bread on time and is happy.

The fakir immediately reached to Shankar without delay, Shankar again did not leave any stone unturned in the service of the fakir, he gave whatever dry food was dry to the fakir. This time when the fakir started leaving the next day, this time the fakir had tears in his eyes. "The fakir started saying, oh God, what have you done?" Here Shankar laughed again and started saying, oh fakir, why are you feeling sad. Whatever God does for us, he does it right, some of his message or Sikh is hidden. Which we do not understand and on the contrary start cursing God. Rest is our karma we should give thanks to God and yes time is not always the same

This time of mine will not be the same. When the fakir returned again after some travel, he could not believe what he saw. Shankar had also become a zamindar of the zamindars. On finding out, the fakir came to know that the zamindar with whom Shankar used to work, that zamindar had no children. That zamindar lived alone, so the zamindar gave all this property in the name of Shankar at the time of death, the fakir was very happy now to see these days of Shankar. The fakir went to Shankar and said, may God always keep this blessing of yours. Hearing this, Shankar started laughing again and said, "Fakir, you are still innocent. Hearing this, the fakir was again surprised and asked, "Is this property also not going to exist" Shankar said yes because the wheel of time will turn again.

In this world, nothing ever remains the same forever, change is nature and rule. If something is eternal, immortal and everlasting, then it is our soul and mind. Hearing Shankar's words, the fakir's mind was filled with peace and the fakir left from there.

Here once again the wheel of time turned, after a long time, when the fakir was passing by with his white beard, he saw that Shankar's palace is there! But Shankar! Now he had left this world. The palace was deserted. Spiders had burnt in the palace. Pigeons were gurgling. The sounds of birds flapping their wings were echoing throughout the palace. Seeing all this, a voice echoed in Fakir's mind. Now that fakir started thinking in his mind that how much a person keeps running throughout his life.

Always worried about something or the other, the things for which a person is always suffering, the things behind which a person is always running, whether it is money, fame, respect, any object or love, these things Unhappy if you don't get it, still sad if you get lost or end together, still sad, while most people know that all this is not going to last forever, all these things will change or end one day Will go

This is the reason that in this race, a person loses his own peace. In his heart, the fakir says that Shankar knew about this knowledge.

He was a very settled person. This is the reason that he did not care when there were ups and downs in his life, he was always happy and lived life freely with a relaxed mind. Because this life too has to end one day. So, friends, always remember that whenever you are going through a bad phase in life, then you are surrounded by all the difficulties, then do not be sad and do not worry because by being sad or worrying, your problems will not end but will increase. Therefore, remember God with your heart in bad times, pray, think calmly on solving the problem and always remember one thing,

Time and circumstances are not always the same, they are always changing.

Today is a bad time

So tomorrow will also be a good time.

Today is a good time

So tomorrow bad times will also come.

" आज बुरा वक़्त है,

तो कल अच्छा वक़्त भी आएगा।

आज अच्छा वक़्त है,

तो कल बुरा वक़्त भी आएगा। "

Never get upset thinking about the future,
always learn to live your today whether it is

good or not and don't be sad thinking that if I am happy today then tomorrow will be a bad day. Learn to live every moment, life itself will take you to the right place at the right time.

Anand and a young girl

Lord Gautam Buddha gave the message of love to the whole world that with love you can conquer the whole world. Buddha says hate can be conquered by love. You can conquer the whole world without love. Think for yourself about what do you want from the world, do you want love or hate from everyone. But all of us do not understand the meaning of love and everything becomes opposite. From desire arises love, from ignorance the same love turns into lust and hatred. One day Buddha's disciples went to the village for joyful meditation and they felt thirsty while toning the tree. He went to a well, there was a girl, he asked her to give him water, at first she agreed to give water, but later she turned the pitcher back and refused to give water. She said what happened. I am from my hand that drinking water from my hand will corrupt your religion. Anand said, don't worry about it, give water because drinking water is an act of virtue. Our Guru Buddha says that there is no high or low on this earth, all are equal. Hearing this, the girl was very happy and gave them water, after that the girl left from there, she kept thinking about Anand on the way.

She liked his thinking very much. Anand was also beautiful to look at. Anyone would be easily fascinated by him, that young woman was also pulling towards Anand. She used to wait for them near the well every day, if she used to go near that well every day, then the same girl would give her water till now, she only wanted to see them for the rest of her life. But now that desire was growing.

One day Anand did not come to the well, the girl became very upset and went to Buddha's ashram to find out about them.

The girl said to Anand today you did not come to the village for tree plantation.

Anand said today I had some work in the ashram.

The girl said you do not discriminate against caste, will you come to my house to eat?

Anand said, "I will tell this by asking Buddha, if I get his permission, I will definitely come."

Hearing this, the girl became happy and left from there, she did not sleep the whole night that day, she felt that Anand also loved her, so she is coming to her house for dinner. The next day, Anand took permission from the Buddha and went to the girl's house. The girl had prepared different types of food for her, Anand accepted that food.

After that the girl said to Anand if you do not discriminate between upper and lower caste, then can I speak my mind to you.

Anand said - yes, definitely speak

The girl said I have started falling in love with you, I want to marry you, will you marry me?

Anand heard this and said that love is not a wrong thing, love should be done by everyone, but I cannot marry you. I am a monk. The goal of my life is not to get married. I only want to serve Buddha.

The girl said that I will not stop you from serving Buddha, but I will serve him with you.

Anand said - what you are thinking cannot happen, saying that he got up from there.

Now this love became a cause of pain for the girl. She wanted to get Anand at all costs. When the girl's mother came to know about this, she thought of a way to get her out of there, she said to her daughter, you trust your mother. That will be yours. You invite Anand to eat again, I will mix the medicine for fainting in his food. After that, you marry a Gandharva with him.

The girl said is this right?

His mother said - there is no right and wrong in love.

The next day the girl again went to meet Anand and said - are you angry with me?

Anand said - No, I do not get angry with anyone and you have not done anything that will make me angry.

The girl said - OK, then will you come again to my house for food?

Anand said that I will definitely come with permission from Buddha.

The next day, Anand went to the girl's place for food. The girl served different types of food to Anand, one of them was mixed with the medicine for fainting. Anand fainted as soon as he ate it.

The girl's mother said - "Go now you get married

The girl said - I don't feel right.

The girl's mother says - "If you think right and wrong then you will never be able to get pleasure."

The girl went inside and came out getting ready. As she went to Anand with the garland

At that point, Anand's unconsciousness broke, and saw the girl with a garland near her, the girl was also terrified to see Anand like this

Anand took the girl away and left without saying anything.

The girl could not say anything.

The girl told her mother that because of you, Anand has turned away from me. I consider myself a sinner, I should not have done this. I have committed a great sin, till now they used to drink water from my hand but now they will not even see my face. She kept thinking in this pain the whole night, kept on mourning.

The next morning, she reached Buddha's ashram and told Buddha that I have committed a great sin, you should punish me for that sin.

Buddha smiled and said, Anand told me about you, you have not committed any sin, you have loved.

The girl said but Anand does not love me, now he must be hating me.

Buddha said Anand does not hate you. He doesn't hate anyone, he only loves. You have not yet understood the reality of love.

The love that brings compassion, brings peace around, on the contrary, love that brings anger, greed, cruelty, destroys freedom, brings pain and disturbance in the mind, and does wrong things, it is not called love, it is called lust. There is peace in Anand even today, he is still happy, he was happy to win before meeting you, and he is equally happy today. As much as he used to love you earlier, he still does the same thing today, there is no pain in his mind, and he is not even suffering from any sinful feelings. His love is real.

On the contrary, you look at yourself what you call love

Do you really have real love?

Are you happy?

Do you have peace of mind?

Hasn't your love made you do any wrong?

How happy were you before, look how much pain you are in now, how can you say that you love?

The girl fell at the feet of Gautam Buddha and said - forgive me. You are right, I could not understand love, you should also include me in your union, I also want to know real love. We all love like parents, brothers, sisters, husband and wife, and friends But do we even understand the love we do? In fact, what we have understood as love is nothing but lust. If your love is pushing you towards selfishness, then you should understand that you do not love, it is your personal selfishness, due to which you are pretending to love. Real love teaches not to take but to give and even in giving it, we get positive energy instead of lack. It is said that a mother spends life laughing for her children by suffering all the sorrows but does not allow them to suffer. But can the same mother give the same love to other's children too, if yes then that is the real selfless love and if not then it is also associated with greed Can't call it real love. In genuinely awakened love there would have been no room for greed, or selfishness.

Do you understand the meaning of real love?

www.ingramcontent.com/pod-product-compliance
Lightning Source LLC
Chambersburg PA
CBHW061406160726
47995CB00001B/484